ESSENTIAL LIBRARY OF
THE US MILITARY

★ THE US ★
ARMY

Essential Library

An Imprint of Abdo Publishing | www.abdopublishing.com

ESSENTIAL LIBRARY OF
THE US MILITARY

★ **THE US** ★

ARMY

PRATT

CONTENT CONSULTANT
PETER R. MANSOOR, PHD
GENERAL RAYMOND E. MASON JR. CHAIR
IN MILITARY HISTORY
OHIO STATE UNIVERSITY

www.abdopublishing.com

Published by Abdo Publishing, a division of ABDO, PO Box 398166, Minneapolis, Minnesota 55439. Copyright © 2015 by Abdo Consulting Group, Inc. International copyrights reserved in all countries. No part of this book may be reproduced in any form without written permission from the publisher. Essential Library™ is a trademark and logo of Abdo Publishing.

Printed in the United States of America, North Mankato, Minnesota
042014
092014

THIS BOOK CONTAINS RECYCLED MATERIALS

Cover Photo: US Army
Interior Photos: US Army, 2, 52–53, 54, 56, 59, 67, 69, 76–77, 79, 81, 84, 94, 96; Marty Lederhandler/AP Images, 6–7; Adam Butler/AP Images, 14; Daniel M. Silva/Shutterstock Images, 16–17; North Wind Picture Archives, 23, 24, 27; Bettmann/Corbis, 28–29; AP Images, 33; US National Archives and Records Administration, 36; Mikami/AP Images, 41; Dominique Mollard/AP Images, 43; Photographer's Mate 1st Class Arlo K. Abrahamson/AP Images, 44–45; US Army/AP Images, 47; US Air Force, 50, 61, 64; Carolina K. Smith/Shutterstock Images, 62–63; Saundra Sovick/The Jonesboro Sun/AP Images, 72; Shutterstock Images, 75; Skryl Sergey/Shutterstock Images, 86 (top); Christos Georghiou/Shutterstock Images, 86 (bottom); US Department of Defense, 88–89, 100; Red Line Editorial, 93

Editor: Rebecca Rowell
Series Designer: Jake Nordby

Library of Congress Control Number: 2014932855

Cataloging-in-Publication Data

Pratt, Mary K.
 The US Army / Mary K. Pratt.
  p. cm. -- (Essential library of the US military)
 ISBN 978-1-62403-433-6
 1. United States. Army--Juvenile literature.   I. Title.
 355.00973--dc23

2014932855

CONTENTS

CHAPTER ONE

OPERATION ENDURING FREEDOM

New York City started September 11, 2001, like any other day. The weather was beautiful, and the sky was a clear, deep blue. People across the United States began the day as usual. But within hours, the country was under attack and on the brink of a war in regions halfway around the world.

The catastrophic events began in Boston,
Massachusetts, at 7:59 a.m., when American Airlines
Flight 11 left the city's Logan International Airport for Los
Angeles, California. Ninety-two people were on the plane.
At 8:14 a.m., United Airlines Flight 175 also left Logan for
Los Angeles. That plane had 65 passengers.

Just six minutes later, American Airlines Flight 77 left Dulles International Airport near Washington, DC. Another 64 people were heading to Los Angeles.

Then, at 8:42 a.m., United Airlines Flight 93 left Newark International Airport in New Jersey. Its 44 passengers were on their way to San Francisco, California.

None of the planes arrived at its destination. Every plane also carried hijackers—19 between the four aircraft. The men threatened passengers and crew members with pepper spray and box cutters they had smuggled onboard. The terrorists took control of the planes.

The hijackers on Flight 11 were the first to wreak havoc. They flew their plane into the North Tower of the World Trade Center in New York City at 8:46 a.m. Hijackers on Flight 175 struck the World Trade Center's South Tower

LOSING THEIR OWN ON SEPTEMBER 11

The US Army lost some of its members on September 11, 2001. Five soldiers—members of the US Army reserve forces—were firefighters in New York City. The men rushed into the World Trade Center after the planes crashed into the two towers. When the towers collapsed, 343 New York City firefighters and paramedics died, including the five soldiers.[1] Another reservist who had been working at his civilian job in the World Trade Center's South Tower also died.

A retired army colonel, Rick Rescorla had been awarded a Silver Star for valor in the Vietnam War and was working as the security chief for a company in the South Tower. He guided nearly all of the company's 2,700 employees out of the building but died when he went back in the tower to make sure everyone had gotten out. In addition, the plane that crashed into the Pentagon that day killed 55 military personnel, some of them members of the US Army.[2]

at 9:03 a.m. The attackers on Flight 77 crashed the aircraft into the Pentagon, the headquarters of the US military in Washington, DC, at 9:37 a.m.

Only the hijackers on Flight 93 were unsuccessful in hitting their target. The passengers on the plane learned about the attacks through phone calls with people on the ground. They rushed the hijackers. As passengers overpowered the terrorists, the plane crashed into a field in Shanksville, Pennsylvania. No one on any of the four flights survived. Many more people died at the crash sites. The attacks killed 2,977 people that day.[3] The events also launched the US military into war.

President George W. Bush addressed the nation early that afternoon: "Make no mistake, the United States will hunt down and punish those responsible for these

THE PENTAGON

The Pentagon is the headquarters of the US Department of Defense. The building, named for its five-sided shape, is a national landmark, like the White House and the US Capitol.

The Pentagon was completed in 1943 and serves as the offices for the worldwide command and control of the US armed forces, including the US Army. It is the world's largest low-rise office building, with more than twice the floor space of the Empire State Building and more than 17 miles (27 km) of corridors. Almost 23,000 military and civilian personnel work at the Pentagon. The attacks on September 11 happened on the sixtieth anniversary of the ground-breaking ceremony that marked the start of its construction. The attacks killed more than 100 people at the Pentagon.[4]

THE TALIBAN AND AL-QAEDA

When the United States went to war in 2001, the Taliban ruled Afghanistan and had allowed al-Qaeda to establish a base within the country.

The Taliban drew its members mostly from the Pashtun, an ethnic group living in Afghanistan and Pakistan. They came to power in the 1990s and enforced an extreme form of the Muslim religion that included requirements for men to grow beards and women to completely cover themselves in a robelike garment called a burka.

The members of al-Qaeda, which was formed in 1989 and led by the Saudi expatriate Osama bin Laden, also followed extreme forms of the Muslim faith. But al-Qaeda members came from all over the world.

Both groups promoted the idea of jihad, or holy war, against Western countries, particularly the United States.

cowardly acts."[5] One week later, on September 18, Bush signed a law authorizing the use of force against a terrorist organization known as al-Qaeda, the group responsible for the attacks. The US military focused on Afghanistan, a small, poor country that served as a base for al-Qaeda and its leader, Osama bin Laden.

SPECIAL FORCES TAKE THE LEAD

US leaders believed the only way to defeat al-Qaeda was to deploy troops to Afghanistan to attack the organization on its home turf. The Americans would also have to fight the Taliban, the organization that ruled the nation and supported al-Qaeda. The US military named the mission Operation Enduring Freedom.

The US Army played a critical role in the operation, deploying the Fifth Special Forces Group (Airborne) from Fort Campbell,

Kentucky. The group was ordered to land by helicopter inside Afghanistan, where it would make contact with members of the Northern Alliance, a group of Afghans who were also fighting the Taliban. The goal was to overthrow the Taliban and destroy al-Qaeda.

The US Army began by setting up a base Uzbekistan, which borders Afghanistan to the north. There, the Fifth Special Forces Group joined members of the 160th Special Operations Aviation Regiment (Airborne), or SOAR, and the Air Force Special Operations Command to form the Joint Special Operations Task Force North, or Task Force (TF) Dagger. Colonel John Mulholland commanded the task force.

Soldiers in TF Dagger worked with Northern Alliance commanders in Afghanistan to overthrow the Taliban. Ideally, this would happen before the winter made many areas inaccessible. By mid-October the first teams of TF Dagger had entered Afghanistan. These teams flew in on helicopters at night into mountains that reached up to 16,000 feet (4,900 m). Clouds, rain, sandstorms, and enemy fire made landing dangerous. But the army had equipped the soldiers with the most sophisticated military technology. Special goggles let soldiers see at night, advanced navigation systems guided them, and precision weapons helped them accurately hit their targets.

US soldiers also relied on tactics used by the army for generations. They traveled by truck, marched on foot, and even rode on horseback with members of the Northern Alliance. The Americans battled through enemy rocket attacks and gunfire. And they worked with other US forces, which dropped bombs from planes to help the Northern Alliance capture key Afghan regions from the Taliban during the fall and winter of 2001. The army's actions showed the Taliban and al-Qaeda that US forces could strike anywhere at any time.

SOAR

The 160th Special Operations Aviation Regiment (Airborne), known simply as SOAR, specializes in nighttime operations and pioneered night flight techniques. SOAR uses modified Chinook, Black Hawk, and assault and attack configurations of Little Bird helicopters.

The army seeks only the best-qualified aviators, crew members, and support personnel for SOAR. Army members volunteer for this unit. Once selected, they go through rigorous training focused on combat skills.

Since its start in 1981, SOAR has been part of numerous important military actions.

It participated in Operation Urgent Fury in 1983, when the United States invaded Grenada to restore its government after a military coup. SOAR also took part in Operation Just Cause in Panama in December 1989, when US forces seized the country's military dictator, Manuel Noriega, whom the US charged with drug trafficking. SOAR conducted complicated night missions during Operations Desert Shield and Desert Storm, the military campaigns aimed against Iraq after it invaded Kuwait in 1990. And SOAR has been a continuous presence in Afghanistan and Iraq in the 2000s.

OPERATION ANACONDA

The victories won by the Northern Alliance and US Army Special Forces during the initial months of the war in Afghanistan liberated the country from the Taliban's control. But many Taliban and al-Qaeda members were still free and hiding in the country's remote areas. US leaders decided the special forces groups could not win the fight alone and called up conventional US Army units.

With this decision, the US military launched Operation Anaconda, its first large-scale attack against the Taliban and al-Qaeda in Afghanistan. The army's 101st Airborne Division's Third Brigade directed the operation. The group led several infantry battalions and other units, including US Special Forces and Navy SEAL personnel, as well as Canadian infantry and helicopters.

Operation Anaconda started on March 2, 2002. For the first time, US forces encountered al-Qaeda fighters who were well camouflaged and well positioned in fortified strongholds where they had stockpiled food and ammunition. The al-Qaeda members stood their ground, but in the end they were no match for the high-tech, highly trained US soldiers. By March 16, 2002, Operation Anaconda was over. The US military suffered 97 casualties, including 15 killed.[6] And while the US military did not capture bin Laden at that time, the army-led forces captured or killed scores of al-Qaeda members, including

Soldiers of the 101st Airborne hit the ground in Afghanistan on April 2, 2002, just delivered by a Chinook helicopter to continue the work started by Operation Anaconda.

some of the group's top leaders. And the army's actions helped US and Northern Alliance forces topple the Taliban from power and force al-Qaeda to retreat to Pakistan.

The US Army's actions in Afghanistan were the latest in a long line of military ventures spanning US history.

The army has been fighting for the United States since before it was an independent nation. And more than 200 years later, the army has shown in Afghanistan and elsewhere that it is still ready and able to defend its homeland.

ORGANIZATION OF THE US ARMY

The US Army organizes its members into groups of various sizes. They range in size from a few soldiers to tens of thousands.

Squad	4–10 soldiers
Platoon	3–4 squads (16–40 soldiers)
Company	3–4 platoons (70–200 soldiers)
Battalion	3–5 companies (500–800 soldiers)
Brigade	3 or more battalions (3,000–5,000 soldiers)
Division	3 brigades (10,000–18,000 soldiers)
Corps	2–5 divisions (20,000–40,000 soldiers)
Field army	2–5 corps[7]

CHAPTER TWO
BORN FROM NECESSITY

The US Army began as an underdog. In the 1700s, the ordinary men who lived in the American colonies came together to protect their lives, their families, and their homes. First, they fought the indigenous peoples of North America. Next, they fought for their rights against those who governed the colonies.

Reenactors take part in a battle from the Revolutionary War, portraying some of the colonists who joined forces to become the Continental army.

Men first trained and fought in local groups, banding together in militias in the towns spread across the colonies. Because British soldiers could not protect every community in battles with Native Americans over land use and cultural differences, the colonists assumed this task from the very beginning of Colonial America.

Twelve of the 13 original colonies required men to serve in the militia when needed. Pennsylvania did not have this requirement because the colony was settled by Quakers, a religious group opposed to war.

These militias did not have uniforms or sophisticated weapons. Their members trained and fought in their own clothes, not uniforms, using whatever guns they owned. In time, the colonial militias would fight the British troops who had once helped protect them.

FIGHTING FOR INDEPENDENCE

Over time, the colonists became increasingly upset with British rule. The colonists prepared to fight for independence against the powerful British military. But the colonists were not regular soldiers. They were everyday people, such as farmers and tradesmen, who trained to be ready to fight on a minute's notice. And on April 19, 1775, these minutemen fought the British in the first skirmishes of what would become the American Revolutionary War: the Battles of Lexington and Concord in Massachusetts.

On June 14, colonial leaders in the Continental Congress formed the Continental army from several militia groups gathered near Boston. Congress defined the army's makeup: "Resolved . . . that each company consist of a captain, three lieutenants, four serjeants [*sic*], four corporals, a drummer or trumpeter, and sixty-eight privates."[1] The militia leaders appointed George Washington, a general in the Virginia militia, as commander in chief the next day.

The colonists who supported independence, along with the colonial governments, contributed what they could, but the army was constantly short of money and supplies. The army also had trouble recruiting enough men to fill its ranks. Still, the Continental army managed to engage the British military for eight years, soldiering under privation and difficult conditions before the war was won.

WOMEN IN THE ARMY

Women have served in the army in small numbers since its start. Women were cooks, nurses, and seamstresses during the Revolutionary War and worked in similar roles throughout the eighteenth and nineteenth centuries. Although most women did not wear soldiers' uniforms or work side by side with male soldiers, some women did serve in combat disguised as men or working beside male relatives who were officially part of the army.

One such heroine was Margaret Corbin. In 1776, she participated with her husband, John, in an attack on Fort Washington in New York. She handled the ammunition for the cannon her husband operated. When he was fatally wounded, she took his place on the cannon crew until she, too, was wounded.

Some women worked as spies, including Anna "Nancy" Smith Strong. At her New York farm, she hung laundry on her clothesline to secretly send signals to other spies.

Clara Barton also served in the army. She became famous for her accomplishments as a nurse during the American Civil War (1861–1865). She later became the first president of the American Association of the Red Cross.

After forcing the British to flee from Boston on March 17, 1776, the Continental army suffered defeats in New York and New Jersey. Washington crossed the Delaware River to surprise the British and their Hessian allies in December 1776 and breathe new life into the revolution. In 1777, the Continental army challenged a large British force invading New York from Canada. At Saratoga, the Continental army fought the British and forced an entire army to surrender. This gave patriots throughout the colonies hope the revolution would succeed, and it brought France into the conflict on the side of the revolutionaries. The Continental army's success at the Battle of Saratoga changed the tide of the war.

After several more years of fighting, the Continental army defeated the British once and for all in the Battle of Yorktown in Virginia on October 19, 1781, leading to a peace treaty two years later. After more than eight years of fighting, the war ended. Through the difficult and dedicated work of the Continental army and its militia brethren, the colonies were now an independent country—the United States of America. And the nation soon established a small national military, which included the US Army.

NEW WORK FOR THE NEW ARMY

The Continental army disbanded after the American Revolutionary War. Congress then created a new structure, giving the US Army a single unit that in the 1780s was named the First American Regiment. Soldiers in the regiment were stationed at the fort in West Point, New York, and in outposts along the western frontier. In the two decades after the war, soldiers confronted groups of Americans leading small rebellions against government authority. Along the frontier, the army battled Native Americans who resisted white settlements. The army also led explorations into the vast territory west of the Mississippi River, with the most famous expedition commanded by Captains Meriwether Lewis and William Clark from 1804 to 1806.

THE US CONSTITUTION AND THE ARMY

The US Constitution created a national army that was independent of the state-controlled militias. In practice since 1789, the Constitution also outlined how that army should be controlled and commanded. It divided responsibilities for the force between the legislative and executive branches. Congress has the power to declare war, to raise an army, and to maintain the navy. The president is the commander in chief of all US military forces.

A second war with England started on June 18, 1812. Much of the fighting during the War of 1812 involved naval battles in the Great Lakes and in the Atlantic Ocean, although there was also significant ground fighting between British, Canadian, Native American, and American forces in Canada, on the eastern seaboard, and in the Gulf of Mexico region. On August 25, 1814, British forces invaded Washington, DC, and burned the US Capitol and the White House. The war turned on September 13, 1814, when the US Army and Navy defeated British forces at Fort McHenry, near present-day Baltimore, Maryland. This battle inspired Francis Scott Key to write the "Star Spangled Banner," which was eventually set to music and adopted as the national anthem.

In the Battle of New Orleans—the last significant battle of the war—General Andrew Jackson led US soldiers against a superior British army that sought to capture the city, which the United States had bought from France as part of the Louisiana Purchase in 1803. The Americans defeated the British in battle on January 8, 1815. Ironically, US and British leaders working in Belgium had already signed a peace treaty on December 24, 1814,

THE CORPS OF DISCOVERY

One of the army's most important contributions to US history was the work of the Corps of Discovery. This military venture started in May 1804 when Captains Meriwether Lewis and William Clark led a select group of army volunteers and civilians through the Great Plains and across the Rocky Mountains to the Pacific coast.

President Thomas Jefferson wanted the men to find a water route from the Mississippi River to the Pacific Ocean. Lewis and Clark's expedition traveled from Saint Louis, Missouri, to Oregon and back. The explorers returned to Saint Louis in September 1806 to report their findings. Although the water route Jefferson wanted did not exist, Lewis and Clark's journey opened the West to American settlement. The Corps of Discovery mapped its route across the West, made contact with more than two dozen indigenous tribes, and made a number of important scientific discoveries.

During the War of 1812, General Andrew Jackson led army troops to success in New Orleans, Louisiana.

but news of the treaty did not reach the United States until February.

The army continued to shape the new nation, mapping the frontier and protecting American settlers. The army battled in the Mexican-American War (1846–1848) and helped the United States defeat its neighbor and bring the new state of Texas into the union. The victory led to a great expansion westward, adding 500,000 square miles (1,300,000 sq km) to the United States, stretching from the Rio Grande to the Pacific Ocean. But, little more than a decade later, army soldiers would fight each other.

AN ARMY DIVIDED

Less than a century since gaining its independence, the United States found itself divided. The American Civil War fractured the nation. In December 1860, South Carolina seceded, or broke away, from the United States. Eventually, 11 states would secede and form the Confederate States of America. Among other issues, these states wanted to preserve the right of its citizens to own slaves. The Northern states made up the Union and wanted to keep the nation intact and to end slavery. The war started in April 1861, when forces from South Carolina attacked

Union and Confederate troops fought in Shiloh, Tennessee, in 1862, pitting former comrades against each other.

US Army forces at Fort Sumter, a fortification in Charleston harbor.

The war also split the US Army. Nearly 300 of its approximately 1,000 officers resigned to join the Confederate army of the seceded states at the start of the war.[2] President Abraham Lincoln called for state militias and volunteers to join the Union army.

Men who had once fought for the same army now fought each other. After nearly four years of war and many difficult battles—including Bull Run, Shiloh, Antietam, Gettysburg, Vicksburg, Chattanooga, Petersburg, Atlanta, and Nashville—Union forces overpowered the Confederates and forced them to surrender at Appomattox in April 1865. The war was finally over. The Union and Confederate armies suffered great losses: approximately 620,000 soldiers died, making it the deadliest war ever fought on US soil.[3]

MEDAL OF HONOR

Soldiers who show bravery in combat are eligible for medals, including the Medal of Honor. This is the United States' highest medal for valor in combat. The first Medals of Honor went to sailors and marines in 1861. Soldiers became eligible to receive the medal in 1862, and many received this honor based on actions during the Civil War. Because the Medal of Honor is the nation's highest honor, the military awards it sparingly, bestowing it to those who have performed actions "far and above the call of duty."[4] Recipients' courage must be well documented.

REBUILDING

After the war, the army's strength declined. By 1876 the army reached a low point of 27,000 soldiers.[5] The army stationed troops to guard the American coasts and the border with Mexico. Several thousand were stationed on the Great Plains to control Native Americans and protect white settlers. Soldiers also broke strikes by workers protesting poor work conditions or low pay. African-American soldiers also served in the army during and after the Civil War in segregated units commanded by white officers. On the Western frontier they were nicknamed "Buffalo Soldiers," a term black service members have come to embrace.

At the end of the century, the army's work expanded beyond the United States and its territories. In 1898, the United States declared war on Spain, accusing the country of sinking the US battleship *Maine*

BUFFALO SOLDIERS

The black soldiers who joined the army after the Civil War became part of segregated regiments, separate from white soldiers. In 1866, Congress created six such regiments. The army soon merged them into four black regiments: the Ninth and Tenth Cavalry and the Twenty-Fourth and Twenty-Fifth Infantry. These regiments served in the West, where they participated in the Indian Wars (1850s–1870s). They earned the name Buffalo Soldiers because the Native Americans thought their hair resembled the matted hair of a bison's hide. The Buffalo Soldiers went on to serve with distinction in Cuba during the Spanish-American War (1898), attacking up San Juan Hill alongside future president Theodore Roosevelt.

African-American soldiers helped the United States win the Spanish-American war by fighting in Cuba in 1898.

while it was docked in Havana Harbor in Cuba. The United States defeated Spain in a matter of months. The Spanish-American war ended the last remnants of Spanish colonial rule, with the United States taking control of new territories in the Caribbean and the Philippine Islands in the Pacific. In the process, the US Army had become a global fighting force.

CHAPTER THREE

THE ARMY OF A SUPERPOWER

When the US Army fought on foreign soil during the Spanish-American War, it was only the beginning of the branch's international work. The 1900s would take the army well beyond its homeland as the United States emerged as a world power.

The 1900s took US Army soldiers around the world, including to China at the start of the century, where they fought in the Boxer Rebellion.

In 1900, the army sent troops to China to fight alongside British, French, Italian, Japanese, and Russian troops against Chinese nationalists known as Boxers, who opposed foreigners in their country. The army was victorious in the Boxer Rebellion, but it and the war with Spain exposed many weaknesses as well. These ranged from problems among its commanders to lack of supplies and uncomfortable uniforms for its soldiers.

The army reacted by making improvements. In 1903, it upgraded its rifles from the Krag-Jorgensen to the Springfield, considered the best rifle in the world at the time. The army also acquired machine guns and new cannons. It adopted new technologies, including motor vehicles, telephones, and airplanes, as these were developed in the coming years. The army also reorganized its command structure, making it more efficient and professional. The army continued its service to the nation in many ways. These included overseeing construction of the Panama Canal in the early 1900s. And in 1916, US Army troops launched a disciplinary expedition into

THE ARMY TAKES TO THE AIR

The US Army's Signal Corps established its Aeronautical Division on August 1, 1907. The small department was in charge of the military's use of flying machines, which at that time included mostly balloons. The division started testing airplanes in 1908 and accepted its first airplane on August 2, 1909. On December 8, 1913, the army created the First Aero Squadron, which became the first air combat unit when it was used in Mexico in 1916.

The army's use of airplanes expanded dramatically during World Wars I and II. As the importance of airplanes grew, government leaders realized an independent military branch was needed. The National Security Act of 1947 created the US Air Force, building the force with thousands of army personnel. The army, however, continued to have its own fleet of planes—mostly helicopters, first introduced in combat in the latter stages of World War II and used more extensively in the Korean and Vietnam Wars.

Mexico after Mexican revolutionary Francisco Villa led 1,500 men on a raid into New Mexico.[1]

Even with its improved equipment, reorganization, and growing international experience, army leaders believed the force was not as prepared as it should be. Many leaders, including politicians, also believed the army was too small given the dangers of the Great War, or World War I (1914–1918), then consuming Europe. Reacting to this concern over the army's small size, the US government passed the National Defense Act on June 3, 1916. The law increased the regular army to approximately 288,000 men, aiming to more than double its ranks. They would be organized into 65 infantry, 25 cavalry, 21 artillery regiments, 91 coastal artillery companies, and various service units for support.[2] The law gave the army five years to meet these numbers, but the United States would find itself at war within ten months. When the nation entered World War I, the US Army was far from the size it needed to be for the monumental task at hand.

WORLD WAR I

Europe erupted in war on July 28, 1914, when the Austro-Hungarian Empire declared war against Serbia after a Serbian nationalist assassinated the heir to the throne. The war involved most of Europe. The United States entered combat in April 1917 after Germany declared unrestricted submarine warfare, which gave its submarines authority to attack any ships, including neutral US vessels, on sight.

The United States sent army troops in the American Expeditionary Force (AEF) to fight against German forces in France. The AEF eventually had more than 2 million men under its command.[3] They fought alongside countries such as Great Britain and France as part of the Allied Forces. US Army general John J. Pershing commanded the AEF. Troops faced brutal trench warfare. They charged over barbed-wire-strewn stretches of no-man's-land, facing machine-gun and artillery fire and poisonous gas as they fought to overtake the other side.

The first significant American offensive of the war was the Battle of Cantigny. On May 28, 1918, the US Army's First Division attacked the German forces that had taken control of the French village of Cantigny. By May 30, the Americans secured their position. The victory cost the First Division 1,067 killed, wounded, and missing soldiers.[4] But the Battle of Cantigny showed the Allies and the Germans that US troops were capable fighters, and it boosted American morale by demonstrating the power of its army. It also established that US soldiers would fight under US commanders and not as part of the French and British armies.

The US Army helped the Allies to victory by engaging in deadly combat in the Second Battle of the Marne, at

Saint-Mihiel, and in the Meuse-Argonne Forest. The war ended on November 11, 1918. Of the more than 4 million soldiers who served in the army during the conflict, approximately 106,000 died and almost 194,000 were wounded.[5]

The US Army decreased in size dramatically after the war. The military branch reorganized following the passage of the National Defense Act of 1920, which decreed the force would be made up of the regular army, the National Guard, and the organized reserve. By 1922, the army had considerably fewer members in its ranks

In May 1918, American soldiers fighting at Cantigny, France, defeated the Germans they battled.

than during the war, just 12,000 officers and 125,000 enlisted men.[6] Its numbers would increase dramatically when war erupted in Europe again.

WORLD WAR II

The United States entered World War II (1939–1945) on December 7, 1941, when Japan attacked the US fleet in Pearl Harbor, Hawaii. The army was largely unprepared for war even though it had been expanding rapidly since the German defeat of France in June 1940. Its strength had increased to 1.6 million soldiers.[7] However, the army did not have enough supplies or weapons for its growing ranks. Some soldiers had to train with broomsticks because there

SELECTIVE SERVICE ACT OF MAY 1917

Congress passed the Selective Service Act of 1917 after the United States officially entered World War I. The law required all men ages 20 to 30—later amended to 18 to 45—to register to serve in the military. On June 5, 1917, more than 9.5 million men signed up for the "great national lottery," or draft, in which men would be selected for required military service.[8] More than 24 million men registered for the draft before the war was over.[9] Of them, 2.8 million were drafted for service.[10]

The system was used again when President Franklin Roosevelt signed the Selective Training and Service Act of 1940. The law created the country's first peacetime draft and established the Selective Service System as an independent federal agency. From 1948 to 1973, the government drafted men to fill vacancies when there were not enough volunteers. In 1973, the military became an all-volunteer force. In 1975, the government ended draft registration but reinstated the practice in 1980. Today, US male citizens and all males ages 18 to 25 living in the United States must register with the Selective Service.

were not enough guns. The army quickly made up for its deficiencies, acquiring more men and more equipment. The army deployed soldiers to Europe, Africa, Asia, and the Pacific to fight battles spanning the globe.

One of the most significant events in army history was the landing of troops on the beaches of Normandy, France, on June 6, 1944, an event known as D-day. The landing included more than 5,000 ships, 11,000 airplanes, and 150,000 servicemen.[11] Five US divisions landed on D-day, and 19 in all took part in the subsequent campaign in Normandy. Allied ships crossed the English Channel, bringing the servicemen from England to the coast of France. Troops disembarked from their landing craft into the surf carrying approximately 75 pounds (34 kg) of equipment. From there, the men walked or crawled across the beaches as enemy fire poured down on them. Allied Forces suffered nearly 10,000 casualties that day, with more than 4,000 dead—most of them on Omaha Beach in the US zone of attack.[12] But they successfully captured the beachheads and began the Allied liberation of Europe.

The difficult campaign in Normandy was followed by fighting across northwestern Europe. In December 1944 and January 1945, the US Army fought the largest battle in its history, the Battle of the Bulge, when German forces launched a counteroffensive in the Ardennes Forest. This great US victory destroyed the last mobile reserves of the

In February 1945, officers inspected the first group of African-American Women's Army Corps members stationed overseas, in England.

German army and ensured the enemy's ultimate defeat. And in the Pacific, the US Army fought Japanese forces in the Marshall and Mariana Islands, New Guinea, Okinawa Island, Peleliu Island, the Philippines, and the Solomon Islands. Germany surrendered on May 7, 1945, and then Japan surrendered on September 2, 1945. More than 11 million men and women served in the army during World War II. Approximately 318,000 of them died, and more than 565,000 were wounded.[13]

FIGHTING IN ASIA

The US Army quickly discharged most of its soldiers after World War II. By 1947, it had 684,000 ground troops left on active duty. It also had 306,000 airmen who would become part of the new, independent US Air Force.[14] They would soon return to combat. Within a few years, the United States was at war again, aiding South Korea after North Korea invaded on June 25, 1950. The army sent 591,487 soldiers in ten divisions to Korea and ramped up to a peak of 2,834,000 by 1953.[15] That year, the Korean War ended in a stalemate. Nearly 30,000 US Army soldiers died during the conflict.[16]

The Vietnam War (1954–1975) followed. The United States started sending military advisers to South Vietnam in the late 1950s. The US Army opened its Military Assistance Command Vietnam (MACV) in Saigon

WOMEN SERVE DURING THE WORLD WARS

During World War I, more than 35,000 women served in the US military. Approximately 21,000 of them belonged to the Army Nurse Corps.[17]

In May 1941, the US government established the Women's Army Auxiliary Corps (WAAC) as part of the Regular Army to train women in a variety of roles, including clerk, cook, driver, or typist. They received the same basic rate of pay of $21.00 per month that men received. But women did not receive overseas pay—extra money earned when deployed abroad—or government life insurance. If a WAAC member were killed, her parents could not collect the death gratuity offered to parents of her male counterparts.

In 1943, a new law created the Women's Army Corps (WAC), which was part of the army's reserve force. During World War II, WAC members served in roles that were once primarily open to men. They were weather forecasters, weather observers, electrical specialists, sheet metal workers, control tower specialists, airplane mechanics, photo-laboratory technicians, photo interpreters, and radio mechanics, among other specialties. More than 150,000 women served in the WAC during World War II.[18]

(present-day Ho Chi Minh City), South Vietnam, on February 6, 1962, to provide military personnel—including the newly designated US Army Special Forces, or Green Berets—to advise the South Vietnamese. Their mission was to offer advice to the South Vietnamese as they tried to stop the North Vietnamese from taking over. Many advisers also took part in combat.

In 1965, President Lyndon B. Johnson and his secretary of defense, Robert McNamara, undertook a major escalation of the war by committing US ground forces to the conflict and by initiating a major bombing

GREEN BERETS

One of the most elite fighting groups in the world is the US Army Special Forces, or Green Berets, a name taken from the distinctive green beret worn as part of their uniform. The Green Berets are experts in unconventional warfare, direct action, reconnaissance, and combating terrorism. Their missions often involve rapid, secretive responses to situations that pose a threat to US security.

Often, the Green Berets are the first US military members to respond to trouble. They are skilled in maneuvering through threatening or hostile scenarios that are not considered conventional combat situations. These soldiers usually have skills in foreign languages, customs, and cultures. And they are adept in training and organizing foreign civilians and soldiers who support US objectives. During the war in Afghanistan, the Green Berets helped local Afghan forces support the US-backed government in Afghanistan.

Most soldiers who become Green Berets volunteer for this duty after completing a tour of service in another combat unit. After rigorous testing, they take a series of specialized courses, which can last 34 to 76 weeks depending upon the soldier's prior training and job specialty. Trainees also learn advanced fighting skills and go through survival training.

offensive against North Vietnam. Almost 4.4 million army soldiers served during the Vietnam War, with US military strength in Vietnam peaking at 536,000 troops in 1968. More than 38,000 army soldiers died during the conflict.[19] In January 1973, the United States withdrew its troops from Vietnam. South Vietnam could not prevail without US support and surrendered to North Vietnam in April 1975.

THE COLD WAR

Following World War II, the United States engaged in a struggle for political, economic, and military dominance with the Soviet Union during the Cold War. Germany was a Cold War hot spot, divided into the democratic Federal Republic of Germany in the west and the communist German Democratic Republic in the east.

The US military played a major role in Germany. US troops faced Soviet troops along the Berlin Wall. The Americans represented freedom to those on the other side of the wall and protected the freedom of the people on its west side. US soldiers also stood ready to defend their West German and North Atlantic Treaty Organization allies along the inner-German border.

At one point, US troops in Europe numbered more than 250,000.[20] According to Jack Clarke, a professor at the Marshall Center, "In the 1970s, we had more US soldiers in Germany than were in the entire French Army."[21] With the collapse of the Soviet Union and the reunification of Germany in 1991, such a strong US military presence was no longer needed. US Army forces in Europe declined dramatically. In 2012, the US Army announced plans to reduce the number of troops in Europe by one-quarter—to approximately 30,000—by 2017.[22]

After decades there, such decreases have meant economic losses for the Germans and personal losses for the locals and soldiers who formed friendships. Hans Gritzbach worked as a civilian for the US Army for 39 years, given the job when he arrived as a refugee following World War II. He said of the US Army, "I owe a lot to the Americans. They paved the way for what I am today."[23]

THE GULF WAR

As the United States headed toward the end of another century, the nation found itself again engaged in conflict abroad. This time, it was in the Middle East.

Iraq invaded neighboring Kuwait on August 2, 1990. After building up troops as part of Operation Desert Shield, the US launched Operation Desert Storm on January 17, 1991, joining forces from more than two dozen countries to liberate Kuwait. The army, with its superior attack helicopters and armored vehicles, demonstrated its power. US forces defeated the Iraqi army in a matter of days. More than 780,000 US Army soldiers served during the Gulf War. Of those who served in the war, 224 died.[24]

SOMALIA

In December 1992, the United Nations approved the use of military force to protect workers who were distributing food shipments to Somalis who were starving. US troops, including those from the US Army's Tenth Mountain Division, led the international military operation that also included troops from Australia, Belgium, Canada, France, Italy, Morocco, and Pakistan. The mission for these troops expanded in the fall of 1993, when they were ordered to restore a government in Somalia.

Several Somali groups were fighting amongst themselves, and when the United States took sides in the conflict, Somalis attacked US forces as well. In October 1993, Somalis shot down two army Black Hawk helicopters

Soldiers in the army's Second Armed Division drove Bradley Fighting Vehicles through Saudi Arabia in January 1991 during Operation Desert Storm.

in the city of Mogadishu. That left a band of approximately 100 Army Rangers and Special Forces soldiers fighting in close combat with Somalis in the city.[25]

Soldiers from the army's Tenth Mountain Division and the US Army Rangers fought to rescue their fellow soldiers. What had started as a mission to capture a warlord ended in a 17-hour firefight called the Battle of Mogadishu that left 18 Americans dead and 84 wounded.[26] US forces left the country by the end of 1994. The army, however, was

RANGERS

Officially known as the Seventy-Fifth Ranger Regiment, the US Army Rangers is an agile and flexible force that conducts complex special missions. The group is the world's best light infantry fighting force and specializes in conducting raids and assaults inside territory controlled by the enemy.

Rangers execute missions by day or night, regardless of weather or terrain. And they are experts in deploying for their special combat missions on short notice.

Rangers are always ready for combat. They are mentally and physically tough. Their missions include seizing or destroying areas that are important to the enemy, such as airfields and strategic facilities. Sometimes they capture or kill enemies of the United States. Other tasks involve gathering information about the activities of enemy troops or rescuing civilians and prisoners of war from enemies. On June 6, 1944, as part of the D-day invasion, Rangers scaled the cliffs of Point du Hoc in Normandy to destroy German artillery overlooking the invasion beaches—the most difficult mission imaginable.

Soldiers who are Rangers join willingly, but not every soldier who wants to be a Ranger becomes one. The requirements are as tough as the Rangers. Only half of those the army accepts into Ranger School actually graduate due to the rigorous training regimen.

The gunner in a US Army Black Hawk helicopter was ready to protect a Cobra gunship during a patrol over Mogadishu, Somalia, in October 1993.

not done with its humanitarian work or its work restoring order in foreign countries.

The army completed similar work throughout the 1990s. Peacekeeping and humanitarian work took soldiers to Haiti and then to Bosnia, Macedonia, and Kosovo. The operations the army completed in the late 1900s foreshadowed its missions today.

CHAPTER FOUR
TODAY'S ARMY IN THE WORLD

A s it has throughout its history, the US Army exists to serve the American people. Its main purpose is to defend the United States and guard the country's national interests. To accomplish that, the army trains, organizes, and equips soldiers to carry out missions. Some of those missions take them into battles, others deter

conflict, while still others involve soldiers helping others
in need—at home and abroad. The branch also provides
the logistics and support that let the other military
branches accomplish their missions. In addition, the
army helps civil authorities, such as state governments,
during emergencies.

MISSION STATEMENT

The US Army has defined its mission as "to fight and win our nation's wars by providing prompt, sustained land dominance across the full range of military operations and spectrum of conflict in support of combatant commanders." The army accomplishes its mission two ways. First, it does so by "organizing, equipping, and training forces for the conduct of prompt and sustained combat operations on land." Second, it does so by "accomplishing missions assigned by the president, secretary of defense and combatant commanders, and transforming for the future."[1]

Part of the army's work in the modern world involves aiding other armies. And its operations reflect partnerships the United States forms with others, such as the North Atlantic Treaty Organization and its agreement to help defend South Korea and Japan. Given the army's broad and varied purpose, the United States deploys army troops to many troubled spots around the world, including wars and humanitarian crises.

THE GLOBAL WAR ON TERROR

The army's role shifted again at the start of the 2000s. The attacks of September 11, 2001, launched the United States into a global war on terror. The war began with strikes against al-Qaeda terrorist training camps in Afghanistan on October 8, 2001. The United States then expanded the conflict by invading Iraq on March 19, 2003. The purpose of Operation Iraqi Freedom was to end the reign of Iraqi dictator Saddam Hussein, who was captured on

An army soldier stands next to weapons and ammunition recovered in 2003 during Operation Valiant Strike, part of the war on terror.

December 13, 2003. In Iraq, he was tried and convicted of crimes against humanity and executed by hanging. The war, however, continued as insurgency and terrorism destabilized the country.

The army's active-duty and reserve soldiers, both men and women, fought in Afghanistan and Iraq. They faced brutal combat, harsh weather, and countless dangers, including bombs planted on roads by enemy forces. After almost nine years of war, US troops left Iraq in December 2011. The United States planned to withdraw most of its forces from Afghanistan by late 2014, having captured or killed many of al-Qaeda's top leaders. Elite US military forces, led by Navy SEALs, killed al-Qaeda leader Osama bin Laden in a daring raid in Pakistan on May 2, 2011.

The global war on terror lasted more than a decade. On May 23, 2013, US President Barack Obama declared the war over, even though operations against al-Qaeda continue today. Obama said the military would fight specific groups deemed enemies of the United States, such as al-Qaeda:

> We must define our effort not as a boundless "Global War on Terror" but rather as a series of persistent, targeted efforts to dismantle specific networks of violent extremists that threaten America.[2]

The combat in Afghanistan and Iraq had a significant impact on the US military, including the army. The wars showed how advanced technology could save lives by hitting only specific targets, using bombs guided by computers and satellite navigation rather than being guided by gravity to their targets, which is the traditional method used when launching or dropping them. The events also highlighted the many dangers soldiers face from enemy forces. The wars revealed how effective the army could be based on its ultimate weapon—the US Army soldier.

HELPING THOSE IN NEED

While the army continued its focus on fighting and winning the nation's wars in the 2000s, the branch also took on humanitarian missions. That work included

BRIGADE COMBAT TEAM

The US Army is composed of various units. The most important is the Brigade Combat Team (BCT). The BCT is the army's principal ground force element. A BCT is a combined arms organization, consisting of infantry, field artillery, armor, engineers, and other supporting elements.

The army has three main types of BCTs: heavy, infantry, and Stryker. The Heavy BCT is made up of tanks and Bradley infantry fighting vehicles. The Infantry BCT (IBCT) consists mostly of dismounted or dismobile infantry. The Stryker BCT gets its name from its central feature: the Stryker, an armored vehicle that gives it greater firepower than the IBCT.

Each BCT has approximately 3,000 soldiers. It is the smallest combined arms unit that can be committed to combat independently, although it often operates as part of a division. A division, which serves as a tactical headquarters, can control up to six BCTs and supporting units in combat operations.

hurricane relief in the United States and disaster relief abroad.

On October 29, 2012, Hurricane Sandy made landfall near Brigantine, New Jersey. A record-breaking storm, Sandy destroyed large swaths of the New York and New Jersey coasts, submerging parts of the area in water as deep as eight feet (2 m) and stranding people in their homes. Approximately 7,000 National Guard members

In October 2012, members of the army's National Guard gave aid to people in New Jersey who were displaced by Hurricane Sandy.

deployed to help residents after the storm—more than 4,000 of them in New Jersey and New York, the states hit hardest.[3]

The next month, army soldiers went to the Philippines after a powerful typhoon hit the island nation, killing several thousand residents. Approximately 100 soldiers, along with other US military personnel, helped support relief operations, which delivered more than 3 million pounds (1.4 million kg) of equipment and supplies to people affected by the storm.[4]

Whether near or far, army soldiers are ready to assist those in need or to fight to defend their nation. They do this with the help of a variety of equipment and training.

THE NATIONAL GUARD

The state militias of Colonial America continue today as the National Guard. The guard has a dual mission to serve both community and country. The force's members are men and women who have civilian jobs or attend college on a regular basis. They also serve as part-time soldiers who agree to be ready to defend the nation or help protect it in emergencies. Guard soldiers live at home, but they drill one weekend each month and attend a two-week training session each year.

The National Guard serves the state governments and the federal government. Just as those early militias protected their own communities, National Guard units are still deployed to help local towns and cities. Guard units generally work within the states they are based, and any state governor, as well as the president, can call for the guard's help at any time.

Guard members often help residents after natural disaster strikes. National Guard members also deploy with the active-duty army around the world as needed. Guard units can see combat and can also be charged with humanitarian work.

CHAPTER FIVE
EQUIPPED TO SERVE

For centuries, soldiers in the US Army relied primarily
on muskets or rifles in battle. They also used cannons
and, later, grenades, machine guns, tanks, helicopters, and
airplanes. Today, the army takes advantage of a variety of
high-technology tools and weapons.

Infantrymen use a variety of weapons to carry out their missions. These weapons range from small arms, such as pistols and rifles, to machine guns, mortars, and antitank weapons.

Every soldier is capable of handling the army's standard weapon, the M16A2 rifle. Soldiers also train with the M249 Squad Automatic Weapon, the M67 Fragmentary Grenade, and the AT-4 Anti-Armor Rocket during their basic training.

Soldiers often learn to handle other types of weapons, depending on their job in the army. For example, soldiers in infantry and Ranger units use the M4A1 Carbine, a rifle, while others are assigned the M240 machine gun as their primary weapon. Officers and some enlisted soldiers carry M9 pistols. Antitank specialists use the Javelin antitank missile to attack armored targets, while mortar crews use 60 mm, 81 mm, or 120 mm mortars to attack more distant targets.

Rangers fired a 120 mm mortar during tactical training in California in January 2014.

ARMORED VEHICLES

Some of the army's most important equipment comes from its fleet of armored vehicles. In combat, the army relies on two versions of the Bradley Fighting Vehicle, which moves soldiers and can attack ground and air targets with its 25 mm chain gun. The M2 Bradley Infantry Fighting Vehicle is valued for its firepower and as a troop carrier, while the M3 Bradley Cavalry Fighting Vehicle supports missions focusing on reconnaissance and security.

The Stryker armored fighting vehicle is agile, fast, and strong. This vehicle is new to the army's arsenal and is used primarily to transport infantry soldiers into combat. The army uses other versions in a variety of roles, including as mobile assault guns, mortar carriers, fire support, and medical evacuation.

The High-Mobility Multipurpose Wheeled Vehicle (HMMWV), or Humvee, is valuable as a high-powered vehicle that can move on roads or in difficult terrain. It is high off the ground and has four-wheel drive, which allows it to operate in rugged areas. The army can configure the Humvee to carry troops, supplies, or weapons or to serve as an ambulance or scouting vehicle. In Iraq and Afghanistan, the army upgraded its Humvee fleet with armored protection to defend against roadside bomb attacks.

In ground combat, the M1A2 Abrams Tank is the army's heaviest and most capable combat vehicle. It consistently delivers heavy firepower from its 120 mm cannon and three machine guns, and it can work in all kinds of weather, climate, and lighting conditions.

EQUIPPED TO FLY

The army's aviation branch focuses on finding, targeting, and destroying the enemy through fire and maneuver, usually in coordination with ground combat forces.

Soldiers offloaded an Abrams Tank from an air force aircraft during a joint exercise in Colorado.

The army has a variety of helicopters for attacking enemies, gathering information, and transporting troops and supplies. The branch uses the Apache Longbow as an attack helicopter by day or by night. It can fly in most weather conditions. Its thermal sights also allow soldiers to see enemy targets based on their heat signatures—the pattern of heat emitted by engines or bodies—from miles away.

The Black Hawk is an all-purpose assault and transport helicopter. The army uses it to transport troops and supplies and to perform medical evacuation.

The army uses the Kiowa Warrior helicopter for scouting and combat missions because it is small, fast, and easy to maneuver. The aircraft has large windows and laser range-finding equipment to guide Hellfire missiles to targets on the ground.

When it needs to move large numbers of soldiers or supplies, the army relies on the Chinook helicopter because it is built to carry heavy loads. Some Chinooks are

BODY ARMOR

The US Army equips its soldiers with body armor to protect them. The gear is designed to protect the body against bullets and flying fragments. The body armor worn by soldiers in 2013 was called Improved Outer Tactical Vest (IOTV). The IOTV had undergone more than a dozen improvements during its use in the wars in Afghanistan and Iraq. Army scientists and researchers worked to make it lighter, more maneuverable, and more effective. In 2013, the army also developed gender-specific body armor to provide female soldiers proper fit and optimal protection.

configured to carry Special Forces soldiers into difficult terrain on night missions.

Although helicopters are powerhouses of the army's airborne fleet, the branch also relies on airplanes. The C-12 Huron is useful for a variety of missions, from transporting cargo or personnel to performing surveillance. The army uses the C-23 Sherpa for small cargo loads.

DRONES

The army also uses unmanned aerial vehicles known as drones. These unmanned aircraft are robots with visual sensors, navigation systems, and weapons. Pilots on the ground control drones with computers.

The US military uses drones for surveillance and attacks. Drones are beneficial because they require less fuel to operate than traditional aircraft and do not put soldiers in harm's way when they execute their missions.

Drones come in a variety of shapes and sizes. Some of them resemble mechanical model planes in size and appearance and are small enough for a soldier to handle. Some experimental models are as small as bugs.

On September 11, 2001, the army had only a handful of drones. By 2013, it had more than 4,000 of the unmanned aircraft.[1] Some drones are used in combat. Currently, most are used for reconnaissance missions.

SOLDIERS' HIGH-TECH GEAR

Army leaders believe their branch's advanced technology helps make their soldiers the best-equipped fighting force in the world. Some soldiers carry global positioning system (GPS) locators, which calculate a destination using earth-orbiting satellites. GPS helps soldiers determine their location and allows them to navigate without getting lost.

Sergeant Jason E. Gerst launched the RQ-11B Raven, an unmanned aerial vehicle, during Raven training on October 5, 2010.

Long-range communications are highly important to the army. Soldiers communicate through radio and text messages sent via satellite and computers. The latter method allows soldiers to stay in touch with each other almost anywhere on the planet, making it more reliable than radio communications.

Night vision technology allows soldiers to see in the dark of night and in other low-light environments without using flashlights or other light sources the enemy might see and target. Therefore, US soldiers can maneuver

DEVELOPING TALOS

In early 2013, the US Special Operations Command (USSOCOM) asked army researchers to develop a new uniform for soldiers. Military officials envisioned a uniform that would protect infantry members from being shot. They also wanted a uniform that could use computer networking and built-in sensors to give soldiers detailed information about what was happening around them and how their bodies were performing. Military leaders essentially wanted a uniform that would make its soldiers almost superhuman. They called this proposed uniform the Tactical Assault Light Operator Suit, or TALOS.

Plans included 360-degree cameras and sensors to detect injuries and apply a special foam to seal wounds. Ideas included an exterior that could change from liquid to solid in milliseconds to protect soldiers from bullets.

The US Army Research, Development, and Engineering Command (RDECOM) led the project. RDECOM's job was to examine and test technologies from different organizations, companies, government agencies, and academic laboratories to find the high-tech gear that could go into this new uniform. RDECOM planned to identify potential technologies within a year and then decide whether it could have a TALOS ready to test within three years.

Even with all the high-tech gear available, soldiers still rely on basic equipment such as a helmet and body armor for protection.

more stealthily at night and still be able to navigate their surroundings, search for their targets, and identify their enemies.

Even with all its mechanical weapons and equipment, what makes the army a great fighting force is its soldiers. The army recruits and trains young men and women who become its most basic, essential, and capable weapon.

CHAPTER SIX

JOINING AND SERVING

I n 2013, the active-duty army had 557,780 full-time members.[1] The Army Reserve had 205,000 authorized soldiers.[2] And the National Guard had approximately 355,000.[3]

Army personnel fall into one of two categories: enlisted soldier or officer. Enlisted soldiers have

specialized training, responsibilities, and areas of expertise. They are expected to perform specific functions and ensure the success of their unit's mission. Some enlisted personnel are noncommissioned officers, who lead small units and provide assistance to staffs to help manage army organizations.

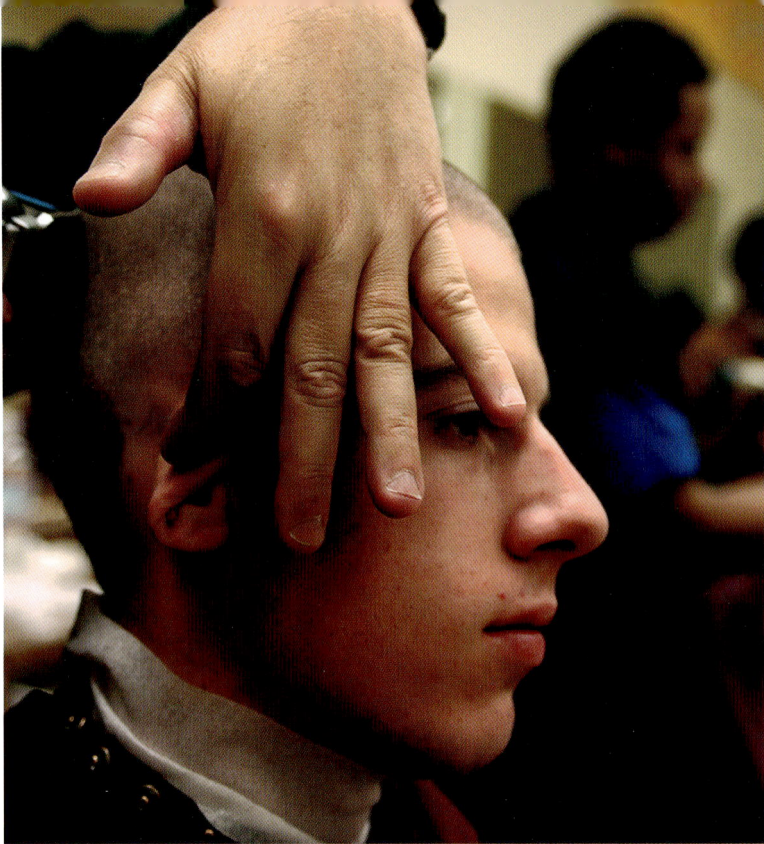

Army recruits at Fort Jackson, South Carolina, get their first haircut as soldiers.

Officers are in charge of overseeing operations. They are leaders and managers. They solve problems, influence others, and make plans the enlisted soldiers follow. To become members of the army, officers had to meet certain requirements established by the military branch.

BASIC REQUIREMENTS

To join the army, a would-be soldier must be 18 to 41 years old. Seventeen-year-olds can enlist if they have parental consent.

Like all branches of the US military, the army has physical and academic standards. In general, potential soldiers need to be in good physical condition and at a healthy weight. They must pass a physical screening before the army will let them join. And they need to be able to meet the physical demands of service. Physical requirements can vary, but the army generally requires potential recruits to "be in good physical condition, of appropriate weight, and able to pass a standard physical screening prior to entry."[4] Potential soldiers must also

SEVEN CORE VALUES

Recruits learn the US Army's seven core values while at boot camp. The army expects its soldiers to live by these values every day, whether they are working at their army jobs or are on their own. The seven values are loyalty, duty, respect, selfless service, honor, integrity, and personal courage.

The army defines loyalty as a soldier being true and faithful to the US Constitution, the army, his or her unit, and other soldiers. Duty means the soldier fulfills his or her obligations in the best way possible. Respect is treating people as they should be treated. According to the Soldier's Code, soldiers "treat others with dignity and respect while expecting others to do the same."[5] Selfless service requires a soldier to put the United States, the army, and any subordinates ahead of his or her own needs. A soldier demonstrates honor by living up to the army's values and integrity by doing what is legally and morally right. Finally, personal courage is facing danger or adversity, whether it is physical or moral.

meet minimum education requirements. The army wants candidates with at least a high school diploma or similar academic credential, such as the general equivalency diploma.

Aspiring recruits need not be US citizens. Immigrants living legally in the United States as permanent resident aliens and other immigrants living legally in the United States may join the branch. Service in the armed forces often leads to citizenship for these soldiers. Residents of US territories, including Guam, Puerto Rico, and the US Virgin Islands are also eligible to join.

ACHIEVING CITIZENSHIP FASTER BY SERVING

Some immigrants can enlist in the US Army. For many years, the army allowed immigrants living legally in the United States as permanent residents to join. In early 2009, the branch adjusted its policy to allow temporary immigrants to join, too. The army wanted to bring on recruits who speak at least one of a variety of languages, including Arabic, Kurdish, and Russian. The army was also interested in recruiting medical specialists. More than 1,000 immigrants enlisted as part of the program through 2013, with the program continuing to draw in immigrants with special skills.[6]

The immigrants must live in the United States for at least two years and must be in the country legally. They must also take and pass an English test. In return for their service, these immigrants could be eligible to become US citizens after six months—a path to citizenship that is much quicker than a typical civilian's wait. The army made the change to attract recruits.

Army recruits completed the low crawl during basic training at Fort Benning, Georgia, in 2012.

BECOMING A SOLDIER

After a would-be soldier has made a commitment to join the army, he or she goes through a series of steps. First, recruits head to a military entrance processing station (MEPS) to finish the enlistment process. MEPS serve all branches of the US military. Here, recruits must show they meet the basic requirements of the military branch they plan to join, which includes undergoing a physical exam.

Recruits also take the Armed Services Vocational Aptitude Battery (ASVAB), a multiple-choice exam that helps determine which career would be a good fit for the test taker. The aspiring soldier also meets with counselors to discuss career options. Before leaving the MEPS, the young man or woman takes the oath of enlistment for his or her particular branch. After the MEPS, the recruit reports to basic training.

All army recruits must complete ten weeks of basic combat training, commonly called boot camp. At boot camp, they go through a general orientation. They get a haircut and uniforms. They then go into training. First, they complete Basic Tactical, followed by Nuclear Biological and Chemical Defense and then Landmine Defense. They learn about US Army heritage and core values. Recruits also take the Army Physical Fitness Test, which will help unit leaders determine each recruit's physical strength.

The next phase includes marksmanship and combat training, as well as learning to rappel at the Warrior Tower. Then, recruits take on additional weapons training and learn how to use automatic weapons and hand grenades. They also put their skills to use at night in the Night Infiltration Course.

Soldiers trained in Grafenwoehr, Germany, in December 2013, using the Dismounted Soldier Training System, a virtual training system.

Finally, recruits take part in graduation. They have transformed from citizens to soldiers.

ADVANCED TRAINING

After boot camp, soldiers go to advanced individual training (AIT). This is where they learn the skills to perform the job they will do for the army. How long a soldier attends AIT, along with what type of AIT is required, depends on the type of military occupational specialty (MOS), or job, the soldier chooses.

Soldiers attend an AIT school for hands-on training and field instruction, where they apply skills under real or simulated job environments. The goal is to make each soldier an expert in his or her given job. There are 17 AIT schools, including Infantry School, where soldiers become experts in combat; Military Police School, where soldiers learn law-enforcement skills; and Signal Corps School, where soldiers learn about communications technology. The careers available to soldiers are in part determined by their test scores for the ASVAB.

BASES WORLDWIDE

Male recruits can expect to complete boot camp at one of five locations: Fort Benning in Georgia, Fort Knox in Kentucky, Fort Leonard Wood in Missouri, Fort Sill in Oklahoma, or Fort Jackson in South Carolina—the largest of all the basic training locations. Where a recruit goes for basic training depends on his or her chosen specialty. For example, Fort Benning provides infantry and cavalry scout training. Fort Leonard Wood offers engineering, chemical warfare, and military police training. And Fort Sill has artillery training. Female recruits are sent to Fort Leonard Wood, Fort Sill, or Fort Jackson, all of which have gender-integrated training. While males and females train together, they do not live together.

After basic training, a soldier may be stationed almost anywhere in the world. The army has posts in 30 states and the District of Columbia. And it has a presence in 74 countries, from Afghanistan to Yemen.[7] The army's locations depend on its duties, which range from humanitarian work to peacekeeping operations to combat missions. As a result, army locations can change at any time.

BECOMING AN OFFICER

Officers take a different path than enlisted personnel. There are two types of officers: commissioned and warrant.

Commissioned officers are responsible for completing missions and ensuring the welfare, morale, and professional development of the soldiers they lead. The army expects these officers to have self-discipline, self-motivation, confidence, and good judgment so they can solve problems and accomplish their missions.

There are four ways to become a commissioned officer. First, college students who enroll in the Army Reserve Officers' Training Corps (ROTC) train during college to become officers and are commissioned as second lieutenants when they graduate.

Second, soldiers who are leaders in certain professional fields, such as law, medicine, and

ROTC

The Reserve Officers' Training Corps (ROTC) started in 1916. The program, which is offered at more than 1,000 US colleges and universities, prepares college students to become officers in the US military. The military often pays for participants' college education and provides a job in the military after commissioning. In exchange, the students promise to serve in the military for four years after they graduate.

The Army ROTC program is considered one of the country's most demanding and successful leadership programs. It gives students leadership development, military skills, and career training. Students take a mix of regular academic classes and army courses, which take place in a classroom and in the field. ROTC students also take part in summer programs with the army.

In May 2012, newly commissioned Arkansas State University–Jonesboro student soldiers helped each other with their officer bars.

religion, can receive a direct commission. This allows these professionals, who include doctors, nurses, and engineers, to become army officers without going through a pre-commissioning training course. Instead, these professionals are commissioned after they complete the officer training program for their specialty.

Third, enlisted soldiers can attend Officer Candidate School (OCS), where they learn the skills needed to become commissioned officers. These soldiers are commissioned as second lieutenants after they graduate from OCS.

Fourth, men and women who graduate from the US Military Academy at West Point, the army's college, enter the army as officers. They also receive commissions as second lieutenants.

The army also has warrant officers, who are highly specialized experts in areas such as piloting helicopters or maintaining vehicles. Warrant officers are different from commissioned officers in that they stay focused on their special areas of expertise for the duration of their careers. Would-be warrant officers attend Warrant Officer Candidate School. The army has 43 technical warrant officer specialties. Areas of expertise include air traffic control, computer technology, counterintelligence, engineering, and food service.

US MILITARY ACADEMY

Following the American Revolutionary War, George Washington and a host of other soldiers and politicians proposed the nation establish a school of war. In 1802, President Thomas Jefferson approved the founding of the US Military Academy, which is known as West Point because of its location in West Point, New York.

Over the years, West Point has modified its curriculum and nonacademic programs, expanding beyond the art and skill of warfare. For example, Douglas MacArthur expanded the school's focus on physical fitness and sports. After serving as a brigadier general in World War I, MacArthur headed West Point. He had seen how demanding war was on the body and wanted cadets to be physically ready for battle. More recently, West Point increased its academic offerings. Today, cadets can major in a variety of fields, including sciences and the humanities.

West Point is open to males and females, the latter of which first entered in 1976. In the 2013–2014 academic year, 4,592 cadets were enrolled at West Point, 16 percent of them female.[8] Recently, engineering and social sciences were the top majors.

LIFE AT THE
US MILITARY ACADEMY

The US Military Academy aims to "educate, train, and inspire" cadets, or students, so they are ready to graduate from college as commissioned officers who can lead according to the army's standards and who can pursue a career as part of the army.[9] The academy does this by providing a college education for free in return for five years of military service. Cadets at West Point, the common name for the academy, can count on being busy. They take classes, study, and play sports like typical college students. They also must fulfill military duties. Cadets also have time for some recreation. Sports are a big part of life at West Point, as one of the academy's mottoes is "Every cadet an athlete."[10] Cadets can also take part in some of more than 100 activities and clubs, ranging from academic clubs—for astronomy and math, for example—to competitive teams for all types of sports.

A typical schedule starts with gathering for breakfast at approximately 7:00 a.m. and attending classes from 7:30 to approximately noon. After an hour or so for lunch, cadets attend classes or study until 4:00 p.m. From 4:15 to 6:30 p.m., they participate in clubs or military or physical training. That is followed by dinner and time for evening study or activities. "Taps," a traditional song played on the bugle, closes the day at 11:30 p.m., with lights out at midnight.

Cadets have the same breaks as other college students. They get time off for Thanksgiving and Christmas. They also get a spring break. However, their summer break is approximately half of the usual college break, with the other half filled with military training.

West Point is different from civilian colleges in other ways, too. Cadets cannot have family or friends visit whenever they want. Cadets have to wear a uniform and behave according to set codes and standards. They must drill and prepare for inspections. They also must take on more and more responsibilities as they move up the cadet ranks at West Point.

West Point cadets march in formation.

CHAPTER SEVEN

CAREER OPPORTUNITIES

T he US Army has two facets: operational and institutional. The operational army performs missions. The institutional army contains the organizations that ensure the readiness of all army forces by training, equipping, and supplying soldiers.

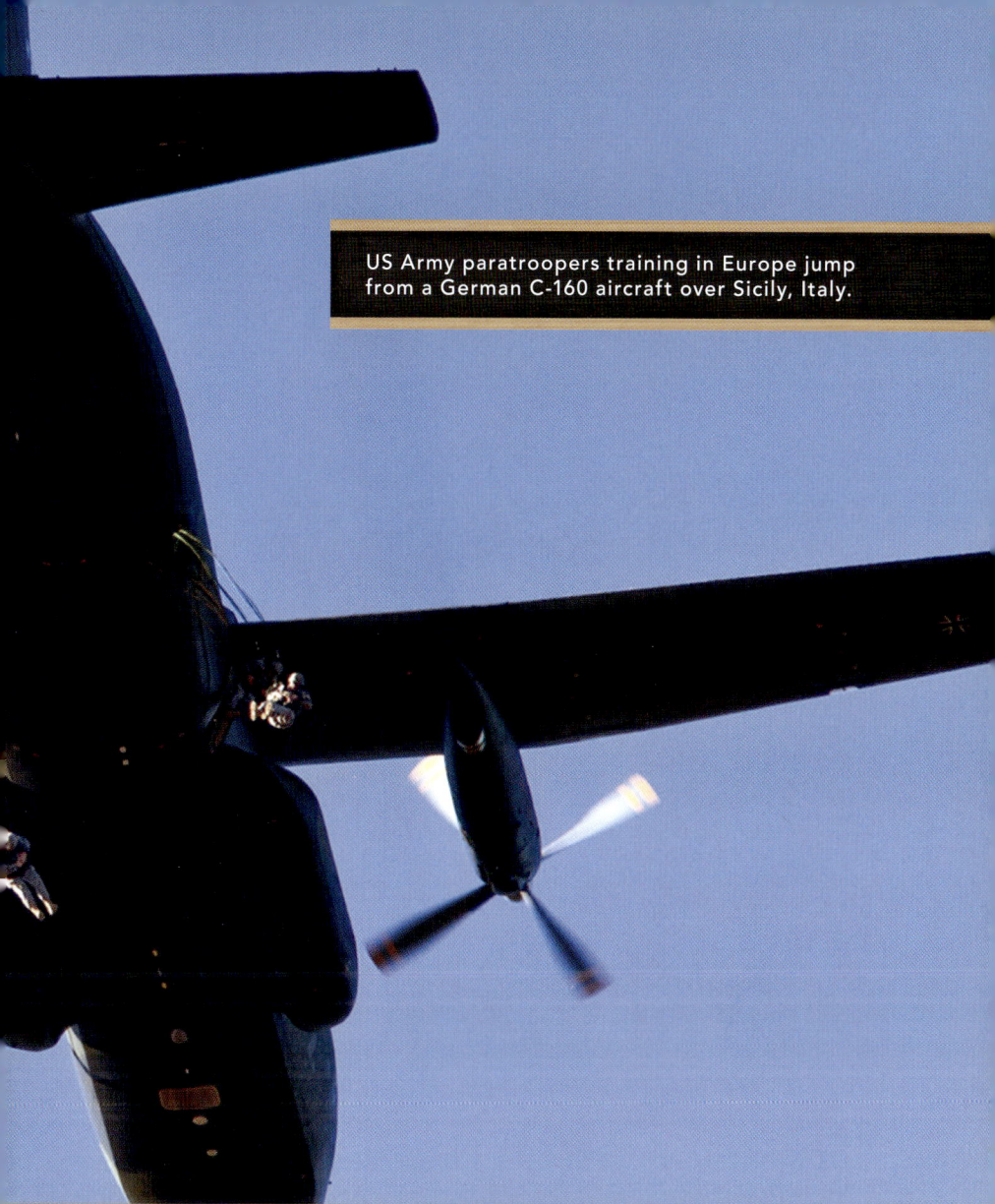

US Army paratroopers training in Europe jump from a German C-160 aircraft over Sicily, Italy.

In short, the institutional army allows the operational army to function.

The army also has two components. One is the active component, made up of full-time soldiers. The other is the reserve component, comprised of the Army Reserve and the Army National Guard, whose members generally serve part-time.

Every member of the army trains for a specific MOS. The army offers more than 150 MOSs. Similar to civilian jobs, army jobs have education, experience, and training requirements. As a result, some positions are open to soldiers in the enlisted ranks. Other positions are open to officers.

ACTIVE DUTY AND ARMY RESERVE

Active-duty soldiers can enlist to serve a term as short as two years to as many as six years, and they are part of the army for the duration of their service term. Active-duty soldiers sometimes deploy overseas on assigned missions that typically last 12 months.

The Army Reserve, on the other hand, allows soldiers to spend most of their time as civilians. Army Reserve soldiers can enlist for terms ranging from three to six years. They work civilian jobs or attend college as if they were not part of the army, but they spend some time every year training with the army at locations near their homes. Usually, reservists spend one weekend each month in army training and two weeks each year attending a field training exercise. The army may call reservists to active duty at any time to fill jobs across the spectrum, normally

Specialist Andrew Dixon, a fire direction specialist, connects chains tying down vehicles to a flat train car.

in times of national emergency. Sometimes the army sends reservists to war zones.

Soldiers who were part of the Army Reserve played a significant role in Afghanistan and Iraq. Reservists became part of the army's fighting forces in both countries, where their contributions were essential for the army.

CAREERS FOR THE ENLISTED

The occupations available to enlisted personnel are extensive. The army breaks down careers into various categories.

In combat operations careers, soldiers work with artillery, infantry, and assault vehicles. Jobs in this area

SPECIALIZED SCHOOLS

Like civilians, soldiers can advance their careers through experience and training. Soldiers who meet certain standards can advance through specialized schools. They teach a variety of skills. Through them, a soldier can become a chaplain, linguist, nurse, parachutist, or one of several other roles.

School	Potential Roles
Airborne	Parachutist
Medical Department School	Nurse, veterinarian
Aviation	Helicopter pilot
Chaplain	Chaplain
Defense Information	Journalist, graphic artist
Defense Language	Interpreter
Drill Sergeant	Drill Sergeant
Judge Advocate General	Attorney
Jumpmaster	Jump expert
Pathfinder	Land navigation specialist
Ranger	Ranger
Recruiting and Retention	Recruiter
Music	Musician
Equal Opportunity Advisors Course	Equal opportunity advisor
Sapper Leader Course	Demolition expert
Special Forces Training	Ranger

Specialist Michelle Metzger, a motor transport driver, performs daily maintenance on a mine-resistant ambush protected vehicle.

include armored assault vehicle crew member and artillery and missile crew member.

In financial and business administration jobs, soldiers can work in accounting, budgeting, and business. Job titles include fiscal chief, finance and accounting specialist, and administrative specialist, which are all crucial to managing the business of the army.

Positions in the arts, communication, and the media are available. In these, soldiers can become musicians in the army band or work as graphic designers, journalists, public affairs specialists, or broadcast technicians who work for the army in publicizing its news.

The army has opportunities in aviation. Aircrew, air traffic controller, engineer, and maintenance specialist are possible jobs in this area. Engineering and scientific careers are also options. Soldiers in these areas may work as meteorological specialists and forecast the weather or space operations specialists, who use and repair the computer systems used to control spacecraft such as satellites.

For those who like to work with people, the army has opportunities as health-care practitioners. Service members assist nurses and doctors while working as

LANGUAGE OPPORTUNITIES

As a military force that operates on a global scale, the army needs soldiers who can speak languages other than English. These soldiers translate news from foreign language newspapers, magazines, radio broadcasts, and other sources. They also work as interpreters, translating written and oral communications. Some serve as interpreters in the field and in offices.

Soldiers who already speak one or more languages besides English can enlist at the rank of specialist and even receive an additional enlistment bonus. Soldiers can apply to learn a foreign language through the US Department of Defense's Defense Language Institute Foreign Language Center, which provides training in 24 languages.

dental specialists, medical care technicians, and physical and occupational therapy specialists.

Computer jobs are available, too. These positions allow soldiers to work as information systems technicians or intelligence/communications division leading chiefs.

CAREERS FOR OFFICERS

Officers also have a variety of career choices. The job categories are similar to those for enlisted members. However, the types of jobs officers have are generally more complex, require higher levels of education and training, and have more responsibilities than those held by enlisted personnel.

Officers in combat operations help manage and coordinate what happens during battle. Their titles include combat mission support officer, field artillery officer, and infantry officer.

WORKING WITH TECHNOLOGY

As a result of all the high-tech gear soldiers now use, the US Army has plenty of technology jobs to fill. The jobs range from positions in communications, where soldiers might handle the encrypted signals that direct missiles or intercept enemy transmissions, to careers in information technology, where soldiers manage the computers and networks that help keep the army running. Other high-tech jobs include engineer, mechanic, and unmanned aerial vehicle pilot. Some soldiers even design video games that are used to train soldiers.

Chief Warrant Officer 4 Robert Cudd, a CH-47 Chinook helicopter pilot, prepares for a mission in Afghanistan.

Aviation jobs are varied. An officer may become an airplane pilot or a helicopter pilot. An officer could also become an air traffic control manager, someone who directs staff on the ground charged with helping guide aircraft to safe landings and takeoffs.

An officer may have a career in business administration and operations careers, where job titles include management analyst and planner or purchasing and contracting manager. People in these positions help direct the business of the army.

Some officers pursue engineering careers, which includes construction and building. Their jobs range from assistant public works officer to civil engineer to facilities officer. Officers in these MOSs help with, among other things, planning facilities and utilities and keeping them operating.

The army also has opportunities in social work and human services. Officers in these areas might serve as chaplains, psychologists, and social workers. Or they could become health-care practitioners, a field that

JUDGE ADVOCATE GENERAL'S CORPS

The US Army Judge Advocate General's (JAG) Corps operates like the army's very own law firm. JAG Corps attorneys are stationed in the United States and overseas. They take on a range of legal cases, from military justice to contract law to international law. These attorneys work as prosecutors and try to put soldiers accused of crimes in jail. They also work as defense lawyers for accused soldiers. Many also provide legal assistance to soldiers, retired army personnel, and their families on personal legal problems. JAG Corps attorneys also represent the interests of the United States on cases in which the army has a stake. Such cases might involve environmental, medical, personnel, or privacy law. Soldiers who want to serve in the JAG Corps must have a law degree and complete the Judge Advocate Officer Basic Course. The course has three phases totaling more than 28 weeks.

US ARMY RANKS

Enlisted Titles

Private
Private 2
←------- Private First Class
Specialist
Corporal
Sergeant
Staff Sergeant ----------→
Sergeant First Class
Master Sergeant
First Sergeant
Sergeant Major
Command Sergeant Major
Sergeant Major of the Army

Warrant Officer Titles

Warrant Officer
Chief Warrant Officer 2 -----→
Chief Warrant Officer 3
Chief Warrant Officer 4
Chief Warrant Officer 5

Officer Titles

First Lieutenant
Captain
←----------------- Major
Lieutenant Colonel
Colonel
Brigadier General
Major General
Lieutenant General
General ---------------→
General of the Army

includes critical care nurses, flight nurses and surgeons, physicians and surgeons, and physician assistants.

Another career option for officers is law enforcement. Options include law enforcement officers, military police, and security officers. Officers specializing in intelligence help gather data and information on enemies and foreign states.

"America's Army represents the full breadth of America's experience. You come from every corner of our country—from privilege and from poverty, from cities and small towns. You worship all of the great religions that enrich the life of our people. You include the vast diversity of race and ethnicity that is fundamental to our nation's strength."[1]
    —President Barack Obama, speech to West Point graduates, May 22, 2010

Through their jobs, army members gain valuable skills. Their training and missions unite them. So, too, does living the army life.

CHAPTER EIGHT

LIFE IN THE ARMY

I n 1981, the US Army ran a television commercial featuring a slogan that defined life in the military branch. The ad proclaimed, "In the Army, we do more before 9:00 a.m. than most people do all day."[1] The commercial captured a real sense of what many soldiers experience.

Army life prepares soldiers for the unexpected through exercises such as the gas chamber.

There is no typical day for a soldier. Daily schedules and expectations are different from soldier to soldier and depend on one's rank and deployment. An infantryman in a war zone will experience a day that is very different than a recruit just starting boot camp or a general working at the Pentagon. But when in garrison, or not deployed, most soldiers begin the day working out, doing physical training before beginning their daily tasks.

At any given time, some army members' days resemble those of an average civilian. They live in communities, drive to work, do their jobs, and then return home. This is not the case for personnel stationed in hostile areas. These service members might patrol enemy territory and face unexpected firefights. Whatever he or she may do on a given day, each and every soldier has taken an oath to defend the United States.

WOMEN IN COMBAT BY 2016

On January 24, 2013, the US Department of Defense announced it was lifting its ban on women serving in combat positions. By 2016, women in all branches of the US military would serve alongside men in battles, along the front lines against enemy forces. Military leaders cited the brave performance of women in Afghanistan and Iraq as proof they could handle combat positions. Nearly 300,000 military women served in Afghanistan and Iraq, and 152 military women died in the two wars. Secretary of Defense Leon Panetta noted of the women, "They serve, they're wounded, and they die right next to each other. The time has come to recognize that reality."[2]

PAY AND BENEFITS

A job as a soldier is similar in some ways to many civilian jobs. The men and women who work as soldiers in the US army receive a salary. The army pays soldiers two types of income. The first is base pay, and the amount a soldier earns is based on his or her rank as well as how much time he or she has served. The second is special

US DEPARTMENT OF DEFENSE BUDGET
FISCAL YEAR 2014[3]

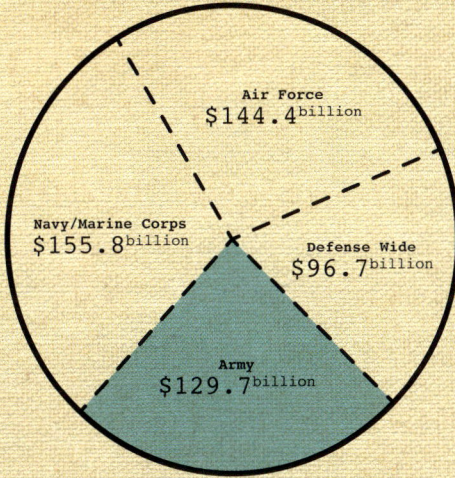

Air Force
$144.4^{billion}$

Navy/Marine Corps
$155.8^{billion}$

Defense Wide
$96.7^{billion}$

Army
$129.7^{billion}$

US ARMY BUDGET FISCAL YEAR 2014[4]

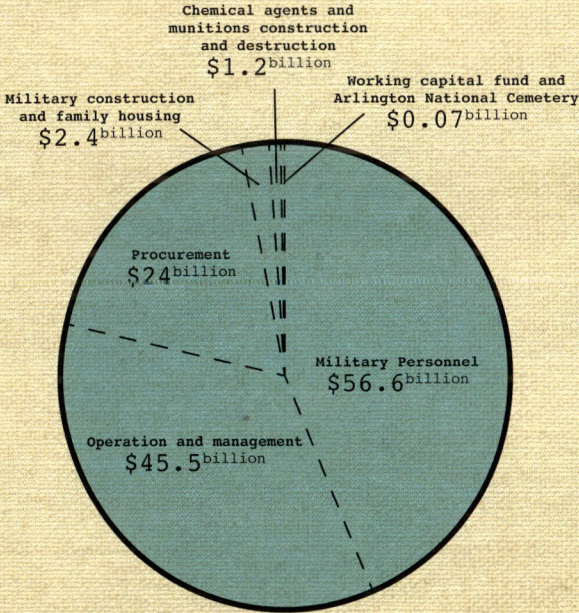

Chemical agents and
munitions construction
and destruction
$1.2^{billion}$

Working capital fund and
Arlington National Cemetery
$0.07^{billion}$

Military construction
and family housing
$2.4^{billion}$

Procurement
$24^{billion}$

Military Personnel
$56.6^{billion}$

Operation and management
$45.5^{billion}$

Numbers may not add up due to rounding.

pay, which is extra money paid based on a soldier's type of service, such as the job and the location where he or she is stationed.

But unlike most civilian workers, soldiers also receive health care and housing and food allowances. The army also gives its soldiers educational opportunities by paying for special training and courses. And active-duty soldiers get 30 days of paid leave, or vacation, each year.

LIFE ON POST

Soldiers move to new duty stations every few years, and the army gives soldiers money to cover moving costs. The army also provides housing for its soldiers.

Unmarried soldiers below the rank of staff sergeant must live on US Army installations. Although the type of

RACIAL INTEGRATION

Today's US Army is an integrated military force, with members from a variety of racial and cultural backgrounds. That has not always been the case. For more than 150 years, the army maintained separate units for whites and blacks. In 1946, the army adopted policies requiring equal rights for black soldiers and an end to segregation based on race but did not implement or enforce them. In October 1948, President Harry S. Truman signed Executive Order 9981, ordering equal treatment of black service members. Integration of military units received a huge boost during the Korean War, when combat commanders needed infantry replacements so much they urged the army to assign black soldiers as replacements. In March 1951, the army's nine training divisions were integrated. In November 1954, the army completed its integration with the deactivation of its last all-black unit, the Ninety-Fourth Engineer Battalion.

ARMY FORTS

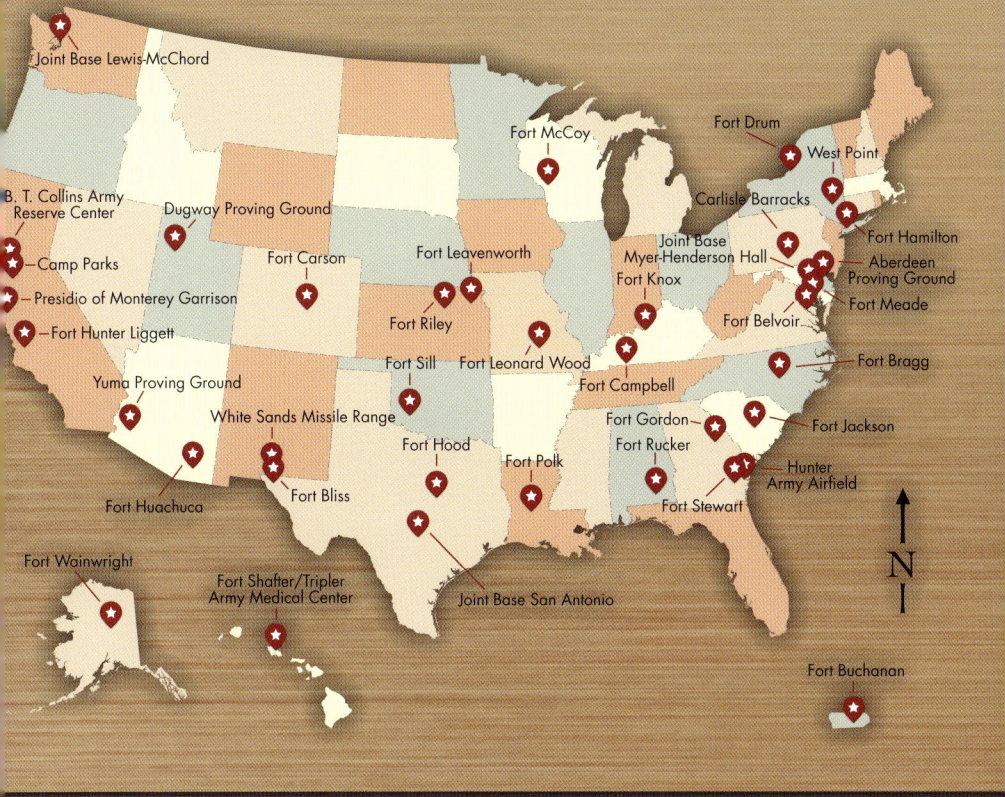

Joint Base Lewis-McChord

B. T. Collins Army Reserve Center

Dugway Proving Ground

Camp Parks

Presidio of Monterey Garrison

Fort Hunter Liggett

Fort Carson

Fort Leavenworth

Fort McCoy

Fort Drum

West Point

Carlisle Barracks

Joint Base Myer-Henderson Hall

Fort Knox

Fort Hamilton

Aberdeen Proving Ground

Fort Meade

Fort Belvoir

Fort Riley

Fort Sill

Fort Leonard Wood

Fort Campbell

Fort Bragg

Yuma Proving Ground

White Sands Missile Range

Fort Hood

Fort Polk

Fort Gordon

Fort Rucker

Fort Jackson

Hunter Army Airfield

Fort Huachuca

Fort Bliss

Fort Stewart

Fort Wainwright

Fort Shafter/Tripler Army Medical Center

Joint Base San Antonio

Fort Buchanan

N

housing available varies according to rank, single soldiers who are just starting out in the army typically live in housing complexes called barracks. These buildings have private sleeping quarters, shared bathrooms, and larger common areas. They resemble college dorms in many ways. Most barracks also have a designated washroom where soldiers can clean their boots, backpacks, and other equipment.

A soldier reads to local children at a story-time event at the base library in Fort Buchanan, Puerto Rico.

Although the army can require married soldiers to live in on-base family housing, usually, they have the choice of living on or off post. If they live on post, they do so in housing that varies from apartments to duplexes to single-family houses, depending on a soldier's rank. Walking trails, playgrounds, and other recreation spaces are often nearby. Soldiers living off post receive a housing allowance.

Soldiers will find army posts resemble small towns where they can find nearly everything they need. A typical army post has stores, libraries, restaurants, movie theaters, and places to worship. Some posts have college facilities. Soldiers are free to come and go from their post, but the security at army facilities differentiates it from coming and going in an average civilian neighborhood. Residents and visitors generally pass through gates guarded by security personnel and must present identification.

COMMUNITY LIFE

The army encourages members and their families to support one another. Army families usually provide a strong network for each other because they often have similar experiences and can help guide each other through the challenges and changes that are unique to the military life and life in the army. For example, an army family whose father or mother is deployed overseas for months can turn to others in the community for support

RESERVE SOLDIER DEPLOYMENT

US Army reservists typically serve one weekend a month and two weeks during the summer. Reservists' time commitment and lives change dramatically when the army activates and deploys them. At that point, reservists become active-duty soldiers—they are soldiers full-time rather than part-time.

The army increases reservists' pay to reflect their full-time work. Reservists also become eligible for additional types of pay, such as a family separation allowance.

Reservists who are activated know the job they left to serve the army full-time is waiting for them back home. Federal law protects their civilian jobs so they can return to work once their active-duty service is completed.

because they have usually experienced that life-changing event, too.

When in garrison and not deployed overseas on missions, soldiers eat typical meals and often sleep in a regular bed. They work when their jobs require it, and they can shop, worship, spend time with family, or just relax during off hours.

CHOOSING TO SERVE

Since the American Revolutionary War, Americans have shown their willingness to defend and protect their land, even before it was officially a nation. From the militia men who became the Continental army to the men and women

Sergeant Irene Lopez returned home from a year in Afghanistan to her loving daughter.

in today's US Army, soldiers have shown they can fight anyone anywhere to defend the United States, its people, its national interests, and its values.

The army has done so by evolving and adapting. The branch integrated women and people of color, incorporated humanitarian work into its missions, and developed technologies to better protect the safety of its soldiers and civilians and complete its missions.

At the same time, the army has given US citizens and noncitizen residents the opportunity to serve the United States in numerous ways, using skills they had when they enlisted as well as those they developed through the rigorous training the army provides. The end result is a fighting force like no other that time and again has shown it can take on any challenge and succeed.

LIFE AFTER THE ARMY

Once a soldier leaves the US Army, he or she may continue working as a reservist. The army also has programs to help support soldiers as they transition from military to civilian life. Every army post has an Army Career and Alumni Program center that helps soldiers prepare for that transition. Career counselors can help soldiers figure out what civilian jobs would use the skills they learned in the army. The counselors also help soldiers as they look and apply for civilian jobs.

TIMELINE

1775

The Second Continental Congress creates the Continental army on June 14.

1775

On June 15, General George Washington becomes the first commander in chief of the Continental army.

1781

The Continental army defeats the British army at the Battle of Yorktown on October 19, the last major fight of the Revolutionary War.

1861–1865

Men who once belonged to the same fighting force battle each other during the American Civil War.

1918

On May 28, the army's Twenty-Eighth Infantry Regiment attacks German forces at Cantigny, France, in the first US offensive of World War I.

1941

In May, Federal law creates the Women's Army Auxiliary Corps.

1944

US Army troops land on beaches in Normandy, France, on June 6, D-day, during World War II.

1954

In November, the army completes its integration of the races with the deactivation of the last black unit in the command, the Ninety-Fourth Engineer Battalion.

1991

US forces invade Iraq beginning January 17, launching Operation Desert Storm.

2001

Elite army forces enter Afghanistan on October 19 in retaliation for al-Qaeda attacks on US targets on September 11.

2011

The last US Army troops leave Iraq in December.

2013

On January 24, the Pentagon lifts its ban on women serving in combat positions in all branches of the military, including the army.

ESSENTIAL FACTS

DATE OF FOUNDING
June 14, 1775

MOTTO
This We'll Defend

PERSONNEL (2013)
Regular Army: 557,780
Army Reserve: 205,000
National Guard: 355,000

ROLE
The US Army's duty is to protect the Constitution of the United States and the freedoms it embodies at home and abroad.

SIGNIFICANT MISSIONS
Battles of Lexington and Concord, Saratoga, and Yorktown, American Revolution, 1775, 1777, 1783
Battle of New Orleans, War of 1812, 1814
Mexican-American War, 1846–1848
American Civil War, 1861–1865
Spanish-American War, 1898
Battle of Cantigny, World War I, 1918
D-day and Battle of the Bulge, World War II, 1944–1945
Korean War, 1950–1953
Vietnam War, 1954–1975
Operation Desert Storm, Gulf War, 1991

War in Iraq, 2003–2011
War in Afghanistan, 2001–present

WELL-KNOWN SOLDIERS

Meriwether Lewis and William Clark led an expedition west as part of the Corps of Discovery to search for a water route connecting the Mississippi River to the Pacific Ocean.

John J. Pershing commanded the Allied Expeditionary Forces during World War I.

Theodore Roosevelt served in Cuba during the Spanish-American War and later became president of the United States.

George Washington was appointed the first commander in chief of the Continental army.

QUOTE

"In the Army, we do more before 9:00 a.m. than most people do all day."—*US Army television commercial, 1981*

GLOSSARY

ARTILLERY
Large firearms, such as cannons and rockets.

CIVILIAN
A person who is not a member of the military.

DEPLOY
To spread out, to place in battle formations.

DISBAND
To break up.

ENLISTED
A member of the armed forces who is not a commissioned officer.

GARRISON
Manning a permanent military base.

INSURGENCY
A rebellion, usually violent.

MILITIA
A group of citizens organized for military service.

NATIONALIST
Someone who believes in and fights for the creation or safety of an independent nation.

RAPPEL
To descend from higher ground or an aircraft using a rope.

STALEMATE
A contest or battle in which neither side is a clear winner.

SURVEILLANCE
Close watch over.

ADDITIONAL RESOURCES

SELECTED BIBLIOGRAPHY

Dorr, Robert F. *Alpha Bravo Delta Guide to the US Army.* Indianapolis, IN: Alpha, 2003. Print.

Gurney, Gene. *A Pictorial History of the United States Army in War and Peace, from Colonial Times to Vietnam.* New York: Crown, 1966. Print.

Morris, James M. *History of the US Army.* New York: Exeter, 1986. Print.

FURTHER READINGS

Giangreco, D. M. *United States Army: The Definitive Illustrated History.* New York: Sterling, 2011. Print.

Hamilton, John. *United States Army.* Edina, MN: ABDO, 2012. Print.

Rose, Simon. *Army.* New York: Weigl, 2013. Print.

WEBSITES

To learn more about Essential Library of the US Military, visit **booklinks.abdopublishing.com**. These links are routinely monitored and updated to provide the most current information available.

PLACES TO VISIT

ARMY WOMEN'S MUSEUM

2100 A Avenue, Fort Lee, VA 23801-2100

804-734-4327/4411

http://www.awm.lee.army.mil

Interactive exhibits and videos tell the story of women's contributions to the army from the American Revolution to the present.

US ARMY HERITAGE AND EDUCATION CENTER

950 Soldiers Drive, Carlisle, PA 17013

717-245-3949

http://www.carlisle.army.mil/ahec

The army's preeminent museum and research complex, is dedicated to educating and preserving the legacy of those who have served as soldiers.

WEST POINT MUSEUM, US MILITARY ACADEMY

2110 New South Post Road, West Point, NY 10996-2001

845-938-2203/3590

http://www.usma.edu/Museum

This museum houses weapons, uniforms, and memorabilia of US soldiers from the seventeenth century to the present and military artifacts from around the world.

SOURCE NOTES

CHAPTER 1. OPERATION ENDURING FREEDOM

1. "9/11 by the Numbers: Death, Destruction, Charity, Salvation, War, Money, Real Estate, Spouses, Babies, and Other September 11 Statistics." *NYMag.com*. New York Media, Sept. 2012. Web. 25 Mar. 2014.

2. Suzanne Summers, William Miller, and Imelda Salazar. "The Role of the Army Reserve in the 11 September Attacks: The Pentagon." *Army.mil*. US Army Reserve Command, 2003. Web. 25 Mar. 2014.

3. CNN Library. "September 11 Anniversary Fast Facts." *CNN.com*. Cable News Network, 11 Sept. 2013. Web. 25 Mar. 2014.

4. Barbara Marazani. "Nine Things You May Not Know about the Pentagon." *History.com*. A&E Television Networks, 15 Jan. 2013. Web. 25 Mar. 2014.

5. "September 11 Timeline: A Chronology of the Key Events that Shaped 9/11." *HuffingtonPost.com*. TheHuffingtonPost.com, 11 Sept. 2013. Web. 25 Mar. 2014.

6. D. M. Giangreco. *United States Army: The Definitive Illustrated History*. New York: Sterling, 2011. Print. 476.

7. "Operational Units Diagram." *Army.mil*. US Army, n.d. Web. 25 Mar. 2014.

CHAPTER 2. BORN FROM NECESSITY

1. "United States Army History: Establishing the Infantry June 14, 1775." *StrategyandWar.com*. Strategy and War, n.d. Web. 27 Dec. 2013.

2. James M. Morris. *History of the US Army*. New York: Exeter, 1986. Print. 65.

3. "American Civil War." *History.com*. A&E Television Networks, 2014. Web. 26 Jan. 2014.

4. "The Medal of Honor." *Army.mil*. US Army, 10 May 2013. Web. 26 Jan. 2014.

5. James M. Morris. *History of the US Army*. New York: Exeter, 1986. Print. 93.

CHAPTER 3. THE ARMY OF A SUPERPOWER

1. Gene Gurney. *A Pictorial History of the United States Army in War and Peace, from Colonial Times to Vietnam*. New York: Crown, 1966. Print. 313.

2. Ibid.

3. Ibid. 204.

4. "Battle of Cantigny." *FirstDivisionMuseum.org*. First Division Museum at Cantigny, 11 Jan. 2014. Web. 25 Mar. 2014.

5. "American War and Military Operations Casualties: Lists and Statistics." *Navy Department Library*. US Navy, Naval History and Heritage Command, 13 July 2005. Web. 25 Mar. 2014.

6. D. M. Giangreco. *United States Army: The Definitive Illustrated History*. New York: Sterling, 2011. Print. 254, 256–257.

7. "US Army Chronology." *Frontline, PBS*. WGBH, 2014. Web. 26 Mar. 2014.

8. "Early Women Soldiers." *Women in the US Army*. US Army, n.d. Web. 7 Dec. 2013.

9. Ibid.

10. Heidi L. W. Golding and Adebayo Adedeji. *The All-Volunteer Military: Issues and Performance*. Washington, DC: US Congress, Congressional Budget Office, 2007. 3. *Google Book Search*. Web. 26 Mar. 2014.

11. "D-Day Overview." *DDay.org*. D-Day Memorial Foundation, 2013. Web. 26 Mar. 2014.

12. Ibid.

13. Anne Leland and Mari-Jana "M-J" Oboroceanu. "American War and Military Operations Casualties: Lists and Statistics." *FAS.org*. Congressional Research Service, 26 Feb. 2010. Web. 27 Jan. 2014.

14. D. M. Giangreco. *United States Army: The Definitive Illustrated History*. New York: Sterling, 2011. Print. 360.

15. "The Korean War 60th Anniversary: Remembering the 'Forgotten' Conflict: Need to Know." *ABC-CLIO.com*. ABC-CLIO, 2011. Web. 26 Mar. 2014.

16. Anne Leland and Mari-Jana "M-J" Oboroceanu. "American War and Military Operations Casualties: Lists and Statistics." *FAS.org*. Congressional Research Service, 26 Feb. 2010. Web. 8 Jan. 2014.

17. "Early Women Soldiers." *Women in the US Army*. US Army, n.d. Web. 7 Dec. 2013.

18. Judith A. Bellafaire. "The Women's Army Corps: A Commemoration of World War II Service." *US Army Center of Military History*. US Army, 17 Feb. 2005. Web. 27 Jan. 2014.

19. Anne Leland and Mari-Jana "M-J" Oboroceanu. "American War and Military Operations Casualties: Lists and Statistics." *FAS.org*. Congressional Research Service, 26 Feb. 2010. Web. 8 Jan. 2014.

SOURCE NOTES CONTINUED

20. "US Military Bases in Germany." *AACVR-Germany.org*. German Historical Institute, Heidelberg Center for American Studies, and Vassar College, n.d. Web. 26 Mar. 2014.

21. Alexandria Hudson. "German Angst as US Troops Bid 'Auf Wiedersehen.'" *Reuters.com*. Thomson Reuters, 27 Jan. 2012. Web. 26 Mar. 2014.

22. US Army Europe Public Affairs. "DOD Announces Plans to Adjust Posture of Land Forces in Europe." *US Army Europe*. US Army, 16 Feb. 2012. Web. 26 Mar. 2014.

23. Andy Eckardt. "Bye, Bye, GI: Deep Impact for Many Germans as US Troops Downsize." *World News*. NBCNews.com, 30 June 2012. Web. 27 Jan. 2014.

24. Anne Leland and Mari-Jana "M-J" Oboroceanu. "American War and Military Operations Casualties: Lists and Statistics." *FAS.org*. Congressional Research Service, 26 February 2010. Web. 8 January 2014.

25. D. M. Giangreco. *United States Army: The Definitive Illustrated History*. New York: Sterling, 2011. Print. 466.

26. "Ambush in Mogadishu." *Frontline, PBS*. WBGH, 2014. Web. 26 Mar. 2014.

CHAPTER 4. TODAY'S ARMY IN THE WORLD

1. "Organization." *Army.mil*. US Army, n.d. Web. 26 Mar. 2014.

2. Paul D. Shirkman. "Obama: 'Global War on Terror' Is Over." *USNews.com*. US News & World Report, 23 May 2013. Web. 7 Dec. 2013.

3. Jim Greenhill. "National Guard Relieves Suffering after Hurricane Sandy." *Army.mil*. US Army, 4 Nov. 2012. Web. 12 Jan. 2014.

4. Howard Reed. "US Sending Additional Military to Aid in Philippines Typhoon Relief." *Stars and Stripes*. US Army, 16 Nov. 2013. Web. 12 Jan. 2014.

CHAPTER 5. EQUIPPED TO SERVE

1. "U.S. Army Unmanned Aircraft Systems Roadmap 2010–2035." *Army.mil*. US Army, n.d. Web. 11 Jan. 2014.

CHAPTER 6. JOINING AND SERVING

1. "Army." *TodaysMilitary.com*. Today's Military, 2013. Web. 7 Dec. 2013.

2. "America's Army Reserve: A Life-Saving and Life-Sustaining Force for the Nation: 2013 Posture Statement." *United States Army Reserve*. US Army, Mar. 2013. Web. 26 Mar. 2014.

3. "ARNG by the Numbers." *Army National Guard*. Army National Guard, 2009. Web. 13 Jan. 2014.

4. "Review Military Entrance Requirements." *TodaysMilitary.com*. Today's Military, 2013. Web. 7 Dec. 2013.

5. "The Army Values." *Army.mil*. US Army, n.d. Web. 26 Mar. 2014.

6. Susanne M. Schafer. "US Army Offers Citizenship Track for Immigrants with Specialized Skills." *HuffingtonPost.com*. TheHuffingtonPost.com, 28 Feb. 2013. Web. 12 Jan. 2014.

7. "About the Army: Post Locations." *GoArmy.com*. US Army, n.d. Web. 7 Dec. 2013.

8. "United States Military Academy." *US News Best Colleges*. US News & World Report, 2014. Web. 26 Jan. 2014.

9. "West Point." *West Point.edu*. Department of the Army, n.d. Web. 26 Jan. 2014.

10. "A Brief History of West Point." *WestPoint.edu*. Department of the Army, n.d. Web. 26 Jan. 2014.

CHAPTER 7. CAREER OPPORTUNITIES

1. "Text of Obama's Speech to West Point 2010 Cadets." *CBSNews.com*. CBS, 22 May 2010. Web. 13 Jan. 2014.

CHAPTER 8. LIFE IN THE ARMY

1. Peter Sattler. "Army 01 1981 US Army Commercial." Television commercial. *YouTube*. YouTube, 9 Feb. 2012. Web. 26 Mar. 2014.

2. Phil Stewart and David Alexander. "Pentagon Lifts Ban on Women in Combat." *Reuters.com*. Thomson Reuters, 24 Jan. 2013. Web. 7 Dec. 2013

3. "Summary of the DOD Fiscal Year 2014 Budget Proposal." *Defense.gov*. US Department of Defense, n.d. Web. 30 Jan. 2014.

4. Karen E. Dyson and Davis S. Welch. "Army FY 2014 Budget Overview." *Army.mil*. US Army, 2013. Web. 30 Jan. 2014.

INDEX

ABOUT THE AUTHOR

Mary K. Pratt is an award-winning freelance journalist based in Massachusetts. She writes for a variety of publications, including newspapers, magazines, and trade journals. She has covered topics ranging from business to technology. In addition to her work, she enjoys spending time with her family and engaging in outdoor pursuits, including running, snowboarding, and skiing.

ABOUT THE CONSULTANT

Dr. Peter R. Mansoor, colonel, US Army (retired), is the General Raymond E. Mason Jr. Chair of Military History at Ohio State University. His 26-year military career included two combat tours in Iraq. He is the author of *The GI Offensive in Europe: The Triumph of American Infantry Divisions, 1941–1945*, winner of the 2000 Society for Military History Distinguished Book Award, and two books on the Iraq War.